The Adventures of Samso

Monica Agnew-Kinnaman

ACKNOWLEDGEMENTS

A great big thank you to my daughter Liz, (also an author) for the many hours spent assisting, advising, and helping me battle an angry computer which does everything in its power to frustrate me.

Another big thank you to my illustrator and friend, Diane Vallejo, whose talented art work brought to life the little animals in this book.

DEDICATION

To the memory of my father, Dr. Samuel Foskett
Ordained minister, physician, author, and dedicated family man.

Chapter 1

This story begins in a quaint little English village called Upper Sawley. Why it bears the prefix "Upper" is a mystery because none of the villagers in living memory has ever heard of a "Lower Sawley." But as Upper Sawley is hundreds of years old nobody really cares.

At the north end of the village, behind high, ivy-covered stone walls, stands a very old castle. The family that inhabits the castle, unlike its illustrious ancestors of several hundred years ago, live in a cluster of rooms beyond the vast entrance hall. The rest of this impressive dwelling is unoccupied except (as rumored by the locals) for a friendly ghost that someone had named George.

It was a warm day in late spring, and as beautiful as only an English spring can be, when Anna started pacing the cobblestones in the castle yard. Anna was six years old with a gray-and-white woolly coat and no tail. In fact, she was a typical Old English Sheepdog, a breed that was often seen in that part of the country. She had been born in one of the castle outbuildings and was a faithful and cherished member of the castle family.

During her lifetime Anna had done her fair share of hard work. In days gone by, when she was young and strong, she had worked side by side with the shepherds in freezing weather after winter storms had swept over the moors, often burying the sheep in deep snow. Anna's dedication and keen sense of smell had saved the life of many a sheep that was lying pinned to the ground by its thick wool coat and a heavy blanket of snow. Unable to move, and hidden from the farmer who was searching for his flock, the sheepdog was its only hope of survival.

But Anna didn't work with sheep any more, or search for them on the freezing moors. Her task had been taken over by the more agile Border Collies who could easily outrun the Old English Sheepdogs, and whose coats didn't become heavy and matted in the winter snows. Consequently Anna had been retired quite happily to a life of ease and comfort on the home farm. On this particular day, however, she was restless and spent her time wandering back and forth in the courtyard.

Laddie, another Old English Sheepdog, appeared in the courtyard and touched noses with her.

"Is it time?" he asked, looking into her soft brown eyes.

"I think so, Lad," Anna replied, licking his face affectionately.

At that moment Ben came around the corner from the barn, carrying two buckets, one in each hand. Ben was the oldest and most valued of the farm workers. His father and grandfather had both worked for the family over several generations, and Ben now lived in a nice little cottage on the estate where he had spent most of his life. Though he was well past middle age, these days he could always be found somewhere around the stables and barns, working with the animals.

"Come wi' me, Anna old gurl," he said kindly, "ah got a grand bed made up for thee in't loose box." Translated, that meant he had a comfortable bed all ready for her in a corner of the stables where horses could move about freely without being haltered. At the moment there were no occupants in the loose box and Anna sank gratefully onto the deep bed of hay covered with a warm blanket, a bowl of clean water by her side. Ben loved all the animals and made sure everybody was comfortable and well cared for.

There was a soft nicker from the adjoining stall and Prince, the huge Clydesdale horse who was now too old to work, stuck his head over the partition.

"How are you feeling, Anna?" he asked with some concern.

"Well, I just wish it was all over," she replied with a sigh, "but thank you for asking."

She laid her head back down on the blanket and tried to rest.

Soon it was evening. As the sun disappeared in a blaze of red and gold, the chickens that had been running around and scratching in the yard went to roost in the hen house, and all the farm animals slept.

Early the next morning, as dawn broke and the rising sun peeped through one of the windows, flooding the stables with its golden rays of light, Prince looked over the top of his stall and gave a soft whinny of delight.

"Well done, little Anna," he said as he admired a black-and-white ball of fur lying nestled against her, then after a moment's hesitation, "but where are all the rest?"

Laddie came through the stable door and greeted Anna affectionately. He gazed at the huge puppy lying beside her, now nuzzling her soft ,warm fur.

"That's a fine boy, but where are all the others?" he asked curiously.

Just then Ben came through the door to lead Prince out to an adjoining meadow where he could have a good roll in the grass and trot around the field if he felt like it. But Ben stopped short when he saw Anna and the new arrival.

"Gaw! Thar's got a right big'un, lass," he said finally, "but wot 'appened to t'others?" (Which, translated, meant, "You have a huge baby, Anna, but where are all the other puppies?")

Anna sighed. Patiently she explained to Lad and Prince, hoping that Ben, too, would understand.

"I know we were all expecting the usual litter of little puppies, but this is *it*," she said firmly. "There aren't going to be any more, and I love this baby just the way he is," and with that she started to lick her puppy tenderly and cuddle him close against her.

At that moment there was a clatter of feet as two little boys and a little girl raced across the courtyard from the castle.

"We heard! Anna's had a baby," one of them shouted excitedly. "Mama, come and see."

The lady of the castle followed them into the stable, and they all gazed admiringly at Anna and her puppy.

"Look how big he is," said the little girl. "What should we call him?"

"How about Giant?" suggested one of the boys, "Or Goliath" said the other.

"I think Samson would be a good name for him," said their mother. "Samson in the Bible was big and strong, and we could call him Sam for short. But we'll see what Daddy says."

Anna thought it was a splendid name for her new baby, and as the children's father agreed that Samson was the perfect name for such a big puppy everything was settled.

*****

It wasn't very long before Samson grew taller and his legs became stronger until he was now able to explore his surroundings. In the early mornings he liked to visit Prince in his stall, crawling about between the great horse's feet until Anna, fearful for his safety, picked him up by the scruff of his neck and carried him back to the loose box. But she needn't have worried because Prince was always careful to stand very still while Samson played on the floor under his tummy, chasing pieces of straw or trying to climb up the horse's feathery legs. He just lowered his head to say, "Good morning, Sam," before continuing to munch his breakfast of oats.

The weeks and months rolled by and Samson grew bigger and bigger until he far surpassed his mother in height and weight. And as he grew, the black baby fur turned to gray, which is the way with Old English Sheepdogs. With his strong body and cute, fuzzy face, he was the picture of health and happiness.

Fortunately Sam was a good son who listened to his mother when she gave him advice or reprimanded him when he was naughty, which was not very often. And Anna told him that as he was so big he must always be gentle and kind to those who were weaker than he. If he came across anyone in trouble or distress, Anna said, he should always try to help them, because that is what good neighbors do.

When winter came, and he was lying cuddled up against her in the warm bed that Ben had made for them, she told him stories. She talked to him of dogs that had done wonderful deeds of courage. She told him about knights in shining armor, mounted on huge fiery steeds that clattered over the drawbridge into this very same castle, hundreds of years ago. They were heroes, she said, who fought evil men and did good deeds, like rescuing damsels in distress. Samson listened spellbound to these tales and decided that one day, when he was old enough and big enough, he was going to be a hero too.

Chapter 2

He was seven months old when Samson began to think how wonderful it would be to explore the world. He wasn't quite sure what the "world" was because he had never been outside the castle grounds, but from the tales his mother told him he knew it had to be more exciting than the home farm where he lived. So one day he made up his mind: he was going to take a walk by himself the very next day and see if he could find the world. When night came he was so thrilled by the idea that he could hardly sleep, and when he dozed off it was to dream of prancing steeds and knights in shining armor.

The next morning he awoke before dawn, while everyone else was still asleep, and quietly crept out of the stables and across the cobbled courtyard. He decided he wouldn't tell anyone else – not even his mother – about what he was going to do. He did feel a little twinge of conscience, but only for a moment. He told himself that he was old enough and big enough to go out into the world by himself and try to be a hero, as long as he was home for breakfast. Samson didn't mean to be disobedient or cause his mother to worry, but he thought to himself, "I will be back before anyone misses me, and besides, nobody ever told me not to go for walks by myself."

So with a happy heart he set off, just as the sun was rising with a rosy glow in the east.

*****

It was a big castle so it took him quite some time to amble around the northern battlements and then follow a narrow, overgrown path to the west. The moat that had encircled the castle centuries ago and the drawbridge that the knights had clattered over into the castle were now long gone. All was quiet and peaceful.

Samson was so intrigued by the new sights and smells he was encountering that he stopped to examine all the exciting new places that he had never had a chance to see before. As he made his way around the far side of the castle he came to an old wooden door that was half open, and as nobody was around he decided to investigate.

The stone steps were old and crumbling, and Sam could see that they led down into a dark basement that looked very scary. He wondered if this was the place where you met the spooks and goblins that the farm animals whispered about when they were gathered together at night, hoping to frighten each other. Standing at the top of the steps he hesitated for just a moment then told himself sternly, "I'm a big boy now and I mustn't be afraid. After all, I'm going to be a hero one day."

Very cautiously he started down the cold, dilapidated steps. Everything was dark and silent. When he reached the bottom he began to wish he had never wanted to be a hero, because at that moment he felt like a very frightened puppy. He shivered a little when he thought of the castle ghost, and wondered if George was going to pop up suddenly and ask what he was doing there.

In the dim shaft of light coming through the half-open door at the top of the stairs he could see that he was in a musty-smelling chamber with old stone walls and a passage leading to somewhere beneath the castle. He heard a slight rustle in a dark corner and his heart nearly stopped beating. Then a rather squeaky little voice said, "It's only me. Don't be afraid, Samson."

Sam froze in his tracks. He stood stock still while trying to peer into the darkness.

"Who are you? And how did you know my name?" he finally managed to ask in rather shaky tones.

"Oh, everyone knows Samson," said the squeaky voice. "I live in the stable where you were born, only I ran away from home today and got lost. I was naughty and my mother was very cross with me. That's why I ran away. And now I am cold and hungry, and I want to go home. I want my mother." The voice broke into loud sobs and there was a sound like someone blowing his nose.

"But you still haven't told me who you are," said Sam, "you don't sound like a dog, and you certainly don't sound big enough to be a horse, like Prince."

"I'm Marty, a mouse. Only a very little mouse, and I'm lost, and frightened. And I don't know how to get home," he sobbed.

"Oh, don't cry. I'll help you," said Sam comfortingly, "but first of all please come out of that dark corner so that we can talk."

Slowly Marty emerged out of the darkness and Samson saw a little creature with a pointy nose, long whiskers, and a thin, hairless tail. Its eyes were filled with tears that dripped over its soft, gray fur onto the ground.

"How on earth did you get in here?" asked Sam gently, feeling a great deal of compassion for the little figure gazing up at him. Now he could see it face to face he realized that Marty looked like all the other mice he had seen in the barns, but none of them ever looked as sad as Marty did at this moment

"I came here through the passage that runs under the castle. It used to lead to the dungeons where they locked people up in the old days, but I couldn't find my way back. And I couldn't climb those stone steps," he blurted out through his tears.

Samson thought for a few moments, then he said cheerfully, "Don't worry, Marty. I'll get you out of here. I will lie down and you can climb up onto my back and I'll carry you outside."

Just at that moment there was a sound that made them both jump.

"Whoooooo," it went. Then again in a higher tone. "Whooooooooo," it wailed. Marty and Samson looked at each other and the hair on the back of Samson's neck began to rise.

"Www-what was that?" whispered Marty in a fearful little squeak. He was trembling so hard he nearly fell over.

"I think it might be George." Sam whispered back, trying to sound brave even though he, too, had gotten an awful fright. "They say this is where he lives."

Then, seeing how terrified the mouse was, he said in a firm voice, "Marty, it's only the wind blowing through the passages." He added quickly, "but let's get out of here all the same."

So he lay down and Marty climbed onto Samson's front leg. By balancing himself with his long tail and digging his little feet into Sam's fur, Marty managed to clamber up onto the sheepdog's back.

Samson rose slowly to his feet, watching over his shoulder to make sure Marty didn't slide off.

"Here we go." he cried. "Hang on!"

And he bolted up the steps and out through the rickety old wooden door into the sunshine where they both breathed a big sigh of relief.

"I wasn't really afraid," said Sam stoutly. "I knew it was just the silly old wind."

"Now, where to, Marty?" he asked, looking over his shoulder to see the little mouse still perched on his back. "I think you should go home because your mother is going to be worried about you."

"Yes," Marty agreed. "I know the way now and I will be home in no time at all. Thank you, Samson. You were very kind to rescue me from that creepy place. I'll never forget you." He gave a soft little nibble on Sam's ear to show his gratitude, then slid down the sheepdog's front leg, landing with a thump on the ground.

"Take care, Marty," said Samson. "and from now on do as your mother tells you," he added sternly, forgetting for the moment that he had left home himself without permission.

Chapter 3

Samson waited until the little mouse was out of sight, then continued on his way down a leafy path until he came to an expanse of blue water rippling in the sunshine. Samson had never seen the lake before as it was on the other side of the castle from the stable where he was born. The most water he had ever seen was the duck pond near the big barn where the ducks serenely floated about, every so often upending themselves so that their tails stuck up in the air as they looked for good things to eat under the water. When he saw the lake he could hardly believe his eyes and he knew this was something he just had to explore.

As he circled the lake he paused frequently to look around and sniff all the wonderful smells that he came across. Sometimes he stopped briefly to roll in the long, sweet-smelling grass that bordered the lake. Everything he saw and smelled was an exciting new adventure for him.

At one point he put a paw gingerly into the water, jumping back in alarm when he went in too far and felt it lapping around his legs. He backed off in a hurry, then feeling rather ashamed of himself he gathered his courage. "You mustn't be afraid. Remember, you are going to be a hero, and heroes aren't afraid of anything."

(At least, that's what he told himself, not knowing that it isn't always true.)

Then, remembering that he had a mission to fulfill, he continued to trot around the lake to see what he could find. He didn't see anybody about and was wondering what to do next when he heard a plaintive little cry. "Help."

"Oh, dear. Someone is in trouble," he thought. "I must see what I can do."

He started searching, all the while calling out, "Where are you? I'm coming."

"I'm here. In the lake and I'm drowning," replied a frantic, teeny little voice.

Sam ran up and down the banks of the lake, but couldn't see anything. He was giving up all hope when he spotted brightly-colored little wings fluttering in the water and a tiny body struggling to keep afloat.

Samson didn't know what this creature was, but it sounded so frightened and so pitiful that he didn't hesitate. He had never learned to swim but when he jumped into the water his legs started to move all by themselves and he found himself paddling clumsily forward - plop, plop, splish, splash. He had difficulty keeping his head out of the water so it got into his mouth and up his nose. He needed to sneeze, but he paddled on, determined not to give up.

Luckily, it was not very far from shore and Sam was soon able to reach the little figure still struggling in the water. Remembering what he had told Marty, he called out, "Hang on to me," and six long, thin legs clutched his fur as he slowly tried to make his way back to the bank. But he was now pointing in the wrong direction! It took more splashing and sneezing and a lot of hard work before he was able to turn himself around, ready to paddle back to dry land.

The beautiful wings drooped sadly and when they were safely on the footpath that circled the lake the little creature was barely able to flutter down to the ground.

It was then, for the first time, Samson realized that he had jumped into the water without knowing how to swim. The very thought of it gave him the shivers and he decided he wasn't even going to go *near* the duck pond when he got home.

He was feeling very tired, so after giving his wet body a good shake he flopped down on his side with his head resting on a tuft of grass. As he was lying there Samson couldn't help looking curiously at the strange little figure next to him, with its thin legs and what appeared to be two horns on its forehead.

"Excuse me, Ma'am," he asked his new friend-in-need, "but what *are* you? I have never seen anything like you before."

"I am a butterfly," she replied. "If it hadn't been for you, I would have drowned. You are very kind and very brave. My name is Beauty and I will tell all my friends how you saved my life."

She started to slowly fold and unfold her exquisite gossamer wings to dry them in the sun.

"Please tell me something about yourself before you go." begged Samson. "I want to know more about the woods, and the fields, and the wildlife folk who live here."

"Well, I will if you'd really like me to," said Beauty, turning round and round as she spoke so that the sun could dry every corner of her wings.

"Before I could become a butterfly," she finally said, in little more than a whisper, "I went through different stages. In one of these stages I was a caterpillar. At that time I was a creepy-crawly thing that most people don't like, even though I am quite harmless. Then one day I escaped from my caterpillar body and became a beautiful butterfly. So now people are kinder to me and forget that I was once a pest that ate the leaves of their plants and trees.

"Why do you have horns on your head?" Sam asked, hoping Beauty wouldn't think it was a rude question.

"These are not horns, my friend. They are called antennae. They help me find my way when I am flying around. I live on nectar that I drink from flowers. There's a meadow on the other side of the lake, and it's full of wildflowers. I was on my way there when a breeze blew me into the water."

Now that her wings were dry and standing up straight Sam could see how beautiful she really was. In fact, he thought she was quite the prettiest thing he had ever seen.

"I must be going now," Beauty said, so quietly that Sam had to bend over to hear her, "but I will never, never forget you." With that she soared up, waving her little antennae in a farewell gesture.

"Goodbye, my dear friend," she called.

Sam was sad to see her go. He lifted a paw to signal goodbye in return, and watched her until she was out of sight.

"Oh well," he sighed, trying to be practical. "If I'm going to be a hero, I had better get on with it."

Chapter 4

As he pressed forward he came to a moss-covered lane that crossed an old pack-horse bridge. He paused to admire the waterfall cascading over the rocks, and to watch minnows and little water bugs swimming in the clear water below. Off to one side there was a murky pool, and a strange-looking green object crouched on a big stone. Samson was fascinated. Eager to know about everything that was going on, he gazed down into the water.

"Hello, there," he called in a friendly voice. "I'm Samson. Who are you and what are you doing sitting on that rock?"

The creature called back in a raspy tone, "I'm Froggy and I'm having lunch. Stop interrupting me and mind your own business."

Just at that moment he gave a big leap into the air and swallowed a bug.

Peering over the bank, Sam saw a tree branch floating in the water and a cluster of stuff that looked like white jelly clinging to it. There were little black specks in the white jelly. Samson was so curious to know more about what he was seeing that he ignored the frog's rude behavior. He called again, "What is that white stuff in the water?"

In a deep, croaky voice the frog shouted back, "Don't you know anything? That's frog spawn, and the black dots are frog's eggs that become tadpoles. The tadpoles grow legs and turn into baby frogs. And now be off with you, you ignorant creature."

Samson was too enchanted by this new world unfolding before his eyes to be offended.

"I wish I could stay and see the tadpoles," he said, "but I have such a lot to do today. You see, I want to find out how to become a hero. I don't suppose *you* could tell me, could you?" he asked hopefully.

"No," croaked the frog, in a cross voice. "I don't know anything about heroes. To tell the truth, I don't even know what a hero is."

Samson refrained from telling Froggy he was ignorant too! Instead, he just said politely, "Well, thank you anyway, sir. It was very nice to meet you."

The frog didn't bother to reply.

Chapter 5

Continuing his journey, Sam crossed over the bridge and was soon in the Bluebell Woods. The scent of thousands and thousands of bluebells floated to his nostrils, and he inhaled deeply. He thought he had never smelled anything so delightful – except perhaps his dinner when he was hungry. As he pressed on he passed a gamekeeper's cottage, deep in the woods. There didn't seem to be anyone around, and it looked so silent and creepy he hurried past and kept going until he was through the woods and into an open, sunlit meadow.

He was standing still, wondering where to go next, when he heard a voice.

"Help! Help!" it gasped. "I'm choking."

Samson looked around him, not knowing where the sound was coming from. There was a hedge surrounding the meadow and he thought something must be hidden there. The cry sounded so plaintive he started off at a gallop, sniffing the air to see if he could find whoever was in trouble. He sniffed all along the hedgerow and listened again for the voice. After a few moments of searching he saw movement and a brown, furry little body lying on the ground. The body seemed to struggle for a few moments, then lay still.

"What is the matter?" asked Samson anxiously, but there was no reply. He crept cautiously towards the small figure lying under the hedge and realized that something was very wrong. There was what looked like a piece of string tied tightly around the little creature's neck, with the other end fastened securely to the ground.

"Oh, how can I help you?" cried Samson.

There was a choking sound and then a whisper. "Please get this thing off my neck. I can't breathe."

Samson realized he had to act quickly. He grabbed the string in his mouth and chewed. In seconds it fell to the ground in pieces, loosening the cord around the creatures neck. There was a sigh of relief as the little animal sat up and took a deep breath.

"Whew! You came just in time or I'd have been a goner."

"Whatever happened to you?" asked Sam, feeling very concerned for the small creature who was now sitting at his feet. "And what was that string doing around your neck?"

"That was a snare," replied the little animal. "Some people put snares in the fields and hedgerows to catch foolish creatures like me. My mother told me not to go in that field, but I didn't listen to her. I'll be a lot more careful now. I don't want to be caught in one of *those* nasty things again."

She gave herself a shake, parting company with the piece of string that was still around her neck, then kicked up her hind legs to show how happy she was to be free. Sam noticed that she had long back legs, very long ears, and a little short white cottony tail that wiggled when she jumped. She thumped on the ground several times with her back feet, then hopped round and round in circles, leaping into the air from time to time. Samson waited patiently until she had calmed down and was lying on her tummy with her back legs stretched out behind her.

"Do you mind telling me what you are?" asked Sam shyly. "I'm meeting so many new friends I'm getting quite confused. You see, I've lived all my life with my mother and Laddie, and all the farm animals. This is the first time I've been away from home by myself and I never knew the world was such a big, scary place."

"My name is Bunny and I'm a rabbit. I live near here in a rabbit warren with a lot of my relatives."

Sam noticed Bunny's nose twitching up and down but was too polite to stare, even though he thought it was rather strange. (You see, he didn't know that bunny rabbits' noses twitch.)

"I'm Samson. I'm an Old English Sheepdog and I live on the other side of Bluebell Woods," replied Sam. "I want to be a hero. A hero is strong and brave like the knights of old who used to go out and do good deeds. Knights used to fight bad people and help good people. And they used to rescue damsels in distress, though I don't really know what that means. But I want to be like them. And if you wouldn't mind my asking," he said, peering around, "what is a rabbit warren?"

He couldn't see any buildings, or a stable where there might be a loose box. There wasn't a blanket or even any hay for a bed, like he had been used to. He knew that the castle horses were in a stable at night, and when it was very cold even the cows liked to keep warm in a shed.

"I'll show you my home," replied Bunny cheerfully. She was now very frisky, hopping around in the grass and sometimes leaping up into the air again. "Follow me."

They didn't travel very far before they came to a place where there were mounds of dirt surrounding holes in the ground. Bunny disappeared down one of the holes, but soon her pert little face was peering out of the opening again, whiskers and nose bobbing up and down.

"This is a warren, and I live here underground with my Mummy and Daddy and a whole lot of other rabbits. It's nice and cozy in the winter, and it keeps us safe from any of the big animals that would like to eat us for dinner. I'm sorry I can't invite you in, but you would never get in the front door, you are so big."

Bunny waggled her whiskers at him, and with a cheerful shout of, "Goodbye. Thank you again," she disappeared into her burrow.

"Well, I couldn't stay anyway," Sam called after her as he turned and trotted off.

"I would like to but I'm going to be very busy. Be careful and don't go near any more snares."

"I'm so glad I was able to help her," he said to himself. But his thoughts soon turned to his task at hand – how to become a hero like the knights of old.

Chapter 6

Sam crossed several fields where cows and horses were grazing, but they were too busy eating to pass the time of day with him. A small flock of sheep ran from him, banding together in a corner of the field where they turned to inspect him. Some of them stamped their feet and opened their mouths, making funny noises that sounded like "B-aaaaa." Samson didn't like to ignore them, but he didn't understand what they were saying anyway so he trotted on, pretending not to notice their rude stares and unfriendly behavior.

He was so engrossed in all the wonderful things he was seeing and the fascinating creatures he was meeting that he didn't even pay attention to where he was going. He just wandered on, enjoying every new experience.

He had traveled quite a long distance from Bluebell Woods when he began to think it would be nice to stop and rest awhile in the shade of some trees. A stream with sparkling water was bubbling over mossy rocks, wending its way through the long grass, and it seemed to be the perfect spot to take a cool drink and spend a few moments relaxing after his long walk.

After a refreshing drink he turned around several times in the lush grass to make a bed. He had just settled himself comfortably, ready to take a short nap, when he heard an ill-tempered voice floating towards him from a nearby clump of bushes.

"What are you doing here?" it asked crossly, "this is my home, not yours. I was in bed asleep and you woke me up."

Samson immediately sat up and tried to see who was addressing him in such an angry manner.

"I'm very sorry," he replied, feeling quite embarrassed. "I didn't know I was disturbing anyone."

There was a snuffling sound behind him and he turned to see a small, very strange-looking creature in the bushes, regarding him with obvious disapproval. Its legs were so short Samson couldn't tell if it was standing up or lying down, and its body was covered with long brown spikes. Besides which it had a sharp little snout, and bright eyes that were closely watching him.

"Well, it isn't really *my* home," said the voice, in milder tones, "I just don't like to be disturbed, that's all. I'm a hedgehog and these fields are my territory."

Samson was captivated by the sight of this unusual creature and wanted to know more about it, but he thought he should introduce himself first.

"I'm Samson, although some people call me Sam," he said. "I'm an Old English Sheepdog and I live with the people who have the castle on the other side of Bluebell Woods. I'm trying to find out how to be a hero. Please tell me more about yourself."

"My, my, you have nice manners. We don't find many like you around here," said the stranger approvingly. "But now you're here I might as well tell you that I have heard about you."

Samson was puzzled.

"How do you know about me?" he asked curiously, "I've never been away from home before."

"Well, if you don't know, I'm not going to tell you," replied the hedgehog curtly, "but we wildlife folk have a way of knowing what goes on in our world.

"However, if you want to know about me there's not a great deal to tell. They call me Prickles because of all these spines on my body. And by the way, I am an old lady, so I prefer to be called *Mrs.* Prickles by a youngster like you. It sounds more respectful."

"Yes, Mrs. Prickles," replied Samson obediently. "But why are you covered in all those sharp spikes?"

"That is for my protection," said Mrs. Prickles. "They don't hurt *me*, but if I am in danger I roll myself into a little ball with all the spines sticking out, tuck my head under, and no one wants to touch me in case they get hurt. These spines can be very painful to my enemies, you know.

"We hedgehogs are nocturnal, which means we are awake at night and sleep during the day. Sometimes we're up and about in the daytime if we are disturbed or very hungry, but we feel safer traveling around when it is dark."

"Another thing that you might like to know is that we sleep in the winter and usually don't wake up until the cold weather is gone. We often sleep in piles of leaves so we hope that no one makes a bonfire while we are hibernating." she said, chuckling.

Samson didn't think that sleeping in burning leaves was very funny but he didn't say anything. He only hoped that people would be more respectful of Mrs. Prickles' home than to light a fire over it.

"We hedgehogs are really very gentle souls and we don't want to hurt anyone as long as no one tries to hurt *us*. I felt safe with you so I didn't take any precautions, like curling myself up into a ball.

Now, if you don't mind, I am going back to bed and try to get some sleep. Good luck, Samson, I hope you find what you are looking for."

"Goodbye, Mrs. Prickles." returned Samson. "Thank you for telling me about yourself."

"What a lot of grand friends I've made today," he said to himself as he trotted off. "And what a wonderful time I'm having."

By now he had forgotten about taking a nap, and when he saw the sun was high in the sky he decided it was time to be getting home as quickly as possible. He was a long way from the castle - and he just remembered that he hadn't told anyone where he was going!

Chapter 7

He turned around and started off the way he thought he had come, but nothing looked familiar. There were no cows or sheep in sight and all the fields seemed to look the same to him. It was very perplexing and poor Samson began to feel anxious and confused.

He had stopped for a moment to try and figure out which way he should go when without any warning he inhaled the most dreadful smell he had ever smelled in his whole life.

"Oh, dear. Whatever can that be?" he gasped, sinking to the ground and covering his nose with both paws. "That's worse than any farm smell."

"Well, it serves you right. You should look where you are going," an indignant voice shouted. "You almost trod on me. And anyway, you should know better than to tangle with a polecat."

"But I didn't see you," protested Samson, "and in any case, I don't know what a polecat is. I only know barn cats."

"Oh, in that case, I'm sorry," said the stranger, now in a softer, refined voice. "I was only defending myself because I thought you were going to attack me. And I am *not* a barn cat. There is no connection whatsoever, I would have you know." He sounded quite offended.

Cautiously Samson uncovered his nose and looked with wonder at the small brown and white animal that was now sitting a few feet away, regarding him with bright, beady eyes.

"I'm Stinky," the little fellow said. "People don't like me because they say I have a very bad smell. I can't help it. That is the way I was born, but at least people keep out of my way when they know I am around, which suits me just fine." He shrugged his shoulders, as if to say he didn't care what people thought.

With that, he gave a flourish of his tail and made for the nearest hedgerow.

"Oh, please wait," Samson called after him. "I didn't mean to be rude. I'd like us to be friends."

Stinky turned around again and sat down, gazing at Sam in astonishment.

"I've never heard anyone say that to me before. Except perhaps another polecat," he added with a rueful grin. "That makes me feel quite proud because both humans and other animals give me a wide berth. They don't want me anywhere near them.

"There are not many of us around here but I understand that in a country called America there are many of our very distant cousins. They are a lot bigger than I am and they don't look quite the same. They're called skunks there, and I've heard that people don't like skunks any more than they do polecats."

"I don't care what anyone else says," Sam assured him. "I think you are very nice, and I would be proud to call you my friend. Now it's getting late and I must find my way home. I would like to stay and talk to you some more but I live on the other side of Bluebell Woods. My name is Samson, by the way, and I want to be a hero like the knights my mother used to tell me about when I was very young."

Stinky looked puzzled. "I'm sorry, Samson," he replied. "I've never heard of knights, but I hope you get to be a hero if that's what you want. It's been a pleasure meeting you, and I hope we'll see each other again." The polecat turned to leave, calling over his shoulder, "I wish I could help you find your way to the Bluebell Woods but I never travel far from home."

"Goodbye, Stinky, my friend. I'll come back and see you again some day." With those parting words the sheepdog set off again, this time at a quick trot even though he still wasn't sure which way he should go.

Chapter 8

After a short while Samson came to a road that he knew wasn't where he wanted to be. There were cars and trucks, all traveling very fast, and Samson became so bewildered he just sat down by the side of the road and wondered what he should do next. He hadn't been sitting there very long when he heard the sound of wings and a beautiful gray dove flew down out of a tree and across the road in front of him. At that very moment a car travelling at a great speed raced around a corner and to Sam's horror hit the bird, knocking her onto the middle of the road. She fluttered down and lay still.

Samson jumped to his feet, forgetting about being lost. "Oh, no!" he cried. "She's going to be crushed by one of those cars. I must try to save her."

As soon as there was a break in the stream of traffic, which luckily was almost immediately, Samson darted out onto the road and picked up the unconscious bird in his mouth. Another car came whizzing around the corner and struck Samson a glancing blow on his shoulder. He fell onto his side and then with great difficulty struggled up onto his feet again. He limped painfully to the side of the road, still carefully holding the warm little body in his mouth.

What should he do next? Then he remembered how a sparrow had flown into a glass window at the castle one day. It lay stunned and motionless on the ground before Ben found it. Gently Ben massaged the tiny body, all the while sprinkling water from the horses' drinking trough on to its head, After a few moments it recovered consciousness and flew away into the bushes.

That's what he had to do now! He remembered the brook where he had tried to rest - until he had been so rudely accosted by Mrs. Prickles - and he knew the place was not very far away. So, with a pain in his shoulder where the car had struck him, and a bleeding front paw, he retraced his steps as fast as he could hobble. Still clasping the bird in his mouth he reached the stream, fervently hoping that Mrs. Prickles was now sound asleep.

He laid the motionless little body down in the grass, and after gathering a mouthful of water he sprinkled drops on the dove's head and tenderly massaged her feathery body with his tongue. After a few moments his efforts were rewarded by a slight movement. The bird moved her legs convulsively and shook her head so vigorously her beak narrowly missed sticking in Samson's ear. After a few moments of floundering about on the ground with wildly flapping wings, she managed to stand up and without a word took off. Flying unsteadily over a nearby hedge she disappeared from view.

"Well, I do wish she had said *something*," Samson reflected. "I would have liked to talk to her and know if she was alright."

Now that he was alone he realized how much pain he was in. His ribs felt on fire and his shoulder hurt where the car had struck him. He licked his front paw, which was still bleeding, but it made him give a little yelp of pain when he tried to stand on it.

The sun, that tells the animals when it's time to go to bed and when it's time to get up in the morning, would soon start to sink in the west, and he was a long way from home. The trouble was that he didn't know where home was. Suddenly he began to feel very sorry for himself. Big tears welled up in his eyes and rolled down his cheeks until there was a little puddle on the ground.

"I'll never get home," he whimpered softly. "I'll never see my mother, or Ben, or the children again. The grownups in the castle will never know that I was only trying to be a hero."

At that moment there was a whirring of wings and the same little gray bird landed beside him. In her gentle dove voice she cooed, "I am *so* sorry. Please forgive my rudeness. With that knock on my head I didn't know what I was doing, and flew away without thanking you for saving my life. I am very, very grateful."

Then, seeing the blood on his paw, with great concern she cried, "Oh, you are hurt! What can I do for you?"

Samson was so glad to see her he stopped crying at once. And to tell the truth he felt embarrassed because he still wanted to be brave like the knights who he was sure would never be caught weeping.

"I'll be all right," he assured her in a very confident voice (even though he was not at all sure that he would be). "I just wish I could find my way home."

"Where do you live?" asked the dove.

"I live in the castle grounds, on the other side of Bluebell Woods. I left home, just for a little while, because I wanted to be like the knights in shining armor who rode big white horses called chargers. My mother said that knights did good deeds and were bold and brave. They even rescued damsels in distress."

He forgot to tell her that he didn't really understand what "damsels in distress" meant, but he poured out his heart to her, confiding all his hopes and dreams as the bird listened patiently.

"My mother told me all about knights. I was going to do daring deeds so she would be proud of me, but now I'm lost and I don't even know how to get home. And my Mum is going to be cross with me, because I didn't tell her where I was going. In fact, I didn't know where I was going myself," he ended sadly.

The dove had never heard of knights in shining armor or damsels in distress and found it all very peculiar, but she listened to what Samson had to say with such sympathy and understanding that it made him feel better right away. Then she told Samson not to worry because she knew where the woods filled with bluebells were. He was just to follow her and she would lead him there.

"My name is Angel," she told Sam. "Of course I am not a *real* angel, but some people say a dove is a symbol of peace and love. Doves are proud to hear that because all we want is for people to be kind to us and to each other.

"If you feel well enough I will lead you to the edge of the woods and show you where the path is that will take you home."

Samson was so pleased at the thought of going home that he jumped up at once, ready to follow his new friend. He couldn't walk very fast because his foot and his side still hurt, but Angel flew in circles above his head, making sure that he could follow her and didn't get lost again. Before evening they had reached the edge of the woods and the path that would take Samson all the way to the old pack-horse bridge and the castle.

Angel flew down beside Sam to thank him again for saving her life. She insisted on giving him an affectionate farewell peck on the nose, and though he winced as her hard beak collided with one of his nostrils, he licked her face in return and said he hoped they would meet again. Then she was gone, winging her way back to her nest several miles away.

Chapter 9

Although Samson was eager to get home to his mother and all the ones who loved him he was disappointed because he felt he had failed in his mission. He had set out that morning with such high hopes and all he had managed to do was get himself lost. And as if that wasn't bad enough, he had been run over by a car and nearly killed. He was just never going to be a hero.

He was so absorbed in his gloomy thoughts that he jumped when he heard a deep voice say, "What are you doing in these woods, Samson?"

He stopped and peered around, the dim evening light making it difficult for him to see. However, he could smell a strange, musky odor which helped him to make out the shape of an animal with reddish colored fur, black legs, and a bushy tail. It was sitting on a tree stump a few yards away, watching him intently. It's appearance seemed vaguely familiar.

"Oh, I didn't see you," exclaimed Sam. "Are you a dog?"

"No, I'm a fox, although I do look rather like some kind of dog, don't I? People sometimes call me Reynard, but I'd rather you just call me Foxy.

I'm not very popular with people around here because occasionally I raid their chicken coops, but I only do that when I can't find anything to eat and I have to feed my family. Then humans come after me with horses, and dogs that they call hounds. Because I have scent glands which give off a strange smell it is easy for them to follow me, so I have to be very careful."

Foxy shifted from a sitting position and lay stretched out on the log with his handsome bushy tail – which, curiously enough, some people call a "brush" - curled around himself.

"Ah, that's better," he sighed as his whole body relaxed, "I was getting quite stiff, sitting here waiting for you. And by the way, I was only teasing. I know who you are and what you are doing here. You live in the castle grounds on the other side of these woods, and you have made friends with Bunny and Mrs. Prickles, and some of the other woodland folk. And I know that you want to do brave deeds so that you can be a hero."

"But *how* do you know?" Sam exclaimed. "Mrs. Prickles knew who I was, too."

"I know everything," said Foxy, with a chuckle and a mischievous grin. "Humans think they are so clever, but they don't realize that we woodland folk are pretty clever too. Anyway, I would like you to tell me about the knights of old, and why you want to be like them."

So Samson lay down beside Reynard, better known as Foxy, and told him about the castle and the knights and the tales his mother used to tell him. Foxy was a very good listener, and asked lots of questions too, just to make sure he understood everything.

"But I still want to know how you heard about *me*," Sam said, when at last he had told the fox everything he wanted to know.

"Have you heard of the bush telegraph? Well, no matter. Humans in some countries use drums to send messages to each other. These messages are heard by one group of people who pass it on to another group of people until everyone from far and wide knows everything that is going on. In the Animal Kingdom it is kind of the same, but our ears are ultra-sensitive and we can hear sounds that no human ear can hear. We don't use drums, of course, and our way of communicating with each other is called the Wildlife Telegraph. When we want to send a message only the wildlife creatures can hear it. We send these messages to other forest creatures and to ones who live in the fields and streams, telling of danger from humans or fires or approaching storms, and all kinds of things. That's how Mrs. Prickles knew about you. Your ears are ultra-sensitive too, and once you are tuned in you will be able to hear us too.

"I heard through the Wildlife Telegraph that you were coming and needed some assistance, so that is why I was waiting for you. I'm here to help you find your way home."

Samson could hardly believe what he was hearing.

"And there is another thing I want you to know," Foxy continued. "all the animals at the castle are safe from us. No fox will ever take a chicken, or eggs, or anything else from there."

Samson was pleased to hear this, but of course he wanted to know why the hens and ducks at the castle were so special.

"Well, first of all let's get you home, and on the way I'll tell you a tale that has been handed down to fox families around here for many years. My grandmother told the story to me and my brothers and sisters when we were just little shavers."

As they both started off at a smart trot, Foxy began his tale.

"Many years ago, when the lady of the castle was a little girl of about thirteen or fourteen she lived in a large manor house on the other side of Bluebell Woods. She loved all the animals, both wild and tame."

"One day, when her parents were away and she was alone with only the servants in the house she heard a commotion in the lane outside the walls surrounding the family dwelling. She heard the baying of hounds and the clattering of horses' hooves. She knew at once what was happening and ran to the front door, just in time to see a fox dragging himself painfully across the lawn, hardly able to move another step. It was obvious that he had run many miles, vainly trying to escape from the hounds and the people on horseback who were chasing him. Now he could run no longer. He managed to reach a small patch of bushes in the garden where he lay down, panting and exhausted as he waited for the end.

"At that moment a very imposing figure, seated on a beautiful chestnut horse and dressed in a scarlet jacket and white riding breeches, came trotting through the big iron gates at the far end of the drive. The Master of Hounds, seeing the young girl in the doorway, rode up until he was directly in front of her.

"Our fox has taken refuge in your garden, Miss. I need permission to bring some of my hounds into your garden and flush him out," the huntsman said in a polite but firm voice, sitting very erect on his horse.

"Confronted by this impressive figure staring down at her from his perch on a great horse and addressing her in such a haughty manner the little girl started to tremble with fright. She had been taught to obey those in authority, but the thought of the terrified creature hiding in the bushes filled her with such sadness she felt as if her heart would break. At first she remained silent, wishing that her father were here so he could tell this man to leave.

Determined not to be thwarted by a child, and starting to lose patience, the huntsman repeated sternly, "I need to bring some of my hounds into your garden and get that fox before he escapes. Are your parents here?"

The child shook her head, then with knees shaking she used every bit of courage she could muster. She drew herself up to her full height of five feet two, hoping to make herself look more impressive, and looked the man straight in the face.

"No, you do not have permission," she replied clearly. " Please keep your hounds out of here."

After some hesitation the huntsman, admitting defeat, touched his whip to his black cap in salute.

"Very well, Miss," he replied. Turning his horse, he rode back down the drive and out through the iron gates. Soon the clattering of hooves and baying of hounds faded into the distance.

For a long time the young girl stood at a window, looking out at the clump of bushes. She would have loved to comfort the poor creature and tell him that he was now safe from harm, but she knew that any human presence would only add to his fears. So she watched and waited.

"Hours later a little red fox, fully refreshed, was seen creeping out of the bushes and making his way home, across the lawn and out of the iron gates. That was my great- great - oh, well I don't know how many great- greats! – but it was one of my great-grandfathers. Many years later, when the little girl was grown up, she married the young lord of the castle beyond Bluebell Woods. And that is why the ducks and geese, and all the hens at the castle are safe from us. There is honor among thieves, you know," he said, with a wink.

Samson was very impressed by this story and told Foxy that he was glad his great-great (however many greats) grandfather was saved, but he was beginning to feel faint from hunger. He hadn't taken time for breakfast and it was now long past his suppertime. He had traveled a long way with only an occasional drink of water from the streams in the meadows and his tummy was starting to rumble.

He looked bashfully at Foxy and said in a small voice, "I'm awfully hungry because I left home early, before Ben had time to give me my breakfast. Do you know anywhere that I could get something to eat?"

"Oh, you poor fellow," said Foxy at once, "we are not far from my home so we'll stop there and get you some food. I always keep a little cache of goodies in my den."

With Samson closely following, he turned off the trail and led the sheepdog deep into the woods to an opening under a fallen tree.

"This is home, sweet home," he told Samson as he crawled under the trunk of the tree and into a large hole he had dug in the ground a long time ago.

"Come on, Sam," he called over his shoulder. "Follow me."

Samson found it was rather a tight fit for him, but he managed to squeeze in after Foxy, and when he got past the entrance he was surprised to find himself in a comfortable living area with a sort of pantry to one side. All kinds of delicious-smelling food was stacked in a corner of the pantry, and Foxy urged Samson to tuck in.

"Come on, Sam old fellow! The Missus is away today, teaching the kids survival techniques, so help yourself. I can always get more."

Samson found the food delicious and, when he had satisfied his hunger, he felt a great deal better. His side wasn't hurting so much any more, and there was only a little dried blood left on his injured paw.

"Mmmmm. That was so good," he exclaimed. "Thank you for sharing your food with me. You are very kind, Foxy. I hope I can do something nice for you one day."

Then he couldn't resist telling his host again how he had wanted to be brave like the knights that used to live in the castle.

"You're a good fellow," the fox said. "And one day you will realize how much we wild folk admire you. But for now we had better get you home before nightfall. I'm going to lead you back to the edge of the woods and show you the path you must follow. It will take you to the pack-horse bridge and the castle. Just watch out for the gamekeeper," he warned, "he's not very friendly and he carries a gun."

When they reached the edge of the woods, the friends touched noses fondly and said goodbye. Foxy bounded away through the trees as Samson trotted off on the woodland path, excited at the thought of home.

Chapter 10

Dusk was fast approaching as Sam hurried through Bluebell Woods. He began to feel a little

nervous and hoped he would reach the pack-horse bridge before night fell. He passed the gamekeeper's

cottage, half-hidden amongst the trees, and again thought how dark and creepy it looked. There were no lights and no signs of life anywhere. Then suddenly a tall figure was standing in front of him and a voice addressed him angrily.

"Hey, you," a man shouted. "what are you doing in these woods, you mangy cur?"

Nobody had ever spoken to Samson like that before and as he sank to the ground, cowering before this rough, ill-tempered human being, he saw a shotgun in the crook of the man's arm.

"You're after the pheasants, I bet, and anything else you can find to chase. Scaring and killing all the wildlife. I know your kind."

To Samson's horror he realized that this was the gamekeeper that Foxy had warned him about! Trembling with fear, he tried to explain that all he wanted to do was rescue damsels in distress like the knights of old, but the man wasn't listening to him.

Sam felt himself grabbed by the scruff of the neck as the gamekeeper hooked his fingers under his collar, and then he was dragged, squirming, towards a shed at the back of the cottage.

"I haven't time to deal with you now, but I will just as soon as I get back," threatened the man. Giving Samson a shove into the dark, cold building he slammed the door shut.

Shaking with fright, Samson began to wonder what "deal with you" meant, but he knew it wasn't going to be good. He heard footsteps fading away as the gamekeeper

strode off into the woods.

While he lay shivering on the dirt floor, Sam tried to think what he could do to escape before this dreadful man returned to carry out his threat. He scratched on the wooden door, but it was locked on the outside. He howled loudly but there was no one to hear him. After about ten minutes of scratching and howling he gave up and resigned himself to the fact that he was a prisoner with no means of escape.

He was still lying miserably, head on paws, when he heard a faint scuffling outside. A whispered voice said through a crack in the door:

"Sam, are you in there? It's Foxy."

Samson leapt to his feet.

"Oh, Foxy," he whispered back. "I'm so glad it's you. I'm frightened. That man said he was going to deal with me when he comes back. What is he going to do to me?"

"Don't worry about that," said the fox with great confidence. "I'm going to get you out of there before he comes back. I'm the best digger in the world."

After saying that he started to dig furiously in the soft earth outside the wooden door of the shed, only stopping long enough to encourage Samson to start digging on his side of the door. Sam set to at once, scraping the dirt floor with his paws and within a few minutes Foxy's nose appeared underneath the rickety old slats. Soon there was a hole just big enough for Samson to wriggle through to freedom.

"Let's go," cried Foxy, and together they started at a gallop, away from the shed and the gamekeeper's cottage. They were on the path leading out of Bluebell Woods, but Samson still felt chills running up and down his spine as he thought of the gamekeeper with his gun and veiled threats.

"What if we meet that awful man again? He has a big gun, remember," he panted as he ran side by side with the fox.

"He's on the other side of the woods now, so you will be quite safe," replied the fox.

When Foxy felt they were far enough away from danger they slowed down.

"How do you know so much?" asked Samson curiously, when he had caught his breath. "You knew the gamekeeper had locked me up in that nasty old shed. And you seem to know where he is now. How do you find out all these things?"

"Do you remember me telling you about the Wildlife Telegraph? Well, one of the night owls has a nest near here and he saw what was going on. He sent a message to Angel, telling her what the gamekeeper had done to you, and she immediately got in touch with me. Now all the creatures in the woods and fields for miles around know what happened to you. And they have been tracking him wherever he goes so that they can let me know. You have a lot of friends here, Sam, and they care about you. I'm going to go with you until you are out of these woods, and I know you won't get into any more trouble."

In no time at all they were out of the Bluebell Woods and crossing the packhorse bridge, where Foxy stopped.

"Goodbye again, young fella. We'll meet again. Take care of yourself."

And he was gone like a puff of wind.

Chapter 11

Dawn was breaking as Samson trotted wearily onto the castle grounds. The sun was peeping over the horizon and the sky lit up again in a blaze of red and gold. Birds were starting to flutter in the trees, and the farm animals waited restlessly for Ben to come and give them their breakfast. The familiar sights and smells that greeted Samson filled him with joy to be back home as he ran to greet his mother and Lad and all the farm animals.

He got such a welcome he was quite overwhelmed. His mother licked his face tenderly and told him how worried she had been, and Laddie, who was always quiet and dignified, ran around like a puppy, filled with joy and excitement to see that Samson was safe. The cows mooed their welcome, and Prince galloped up and down his field, mane and tail flying.

The children, and even their parents, came running out of the castle to see what all the fuss was about. When they saw Samson there were squeals of joy, and the children hugged him and kissed him on the top of his furry head, crying "Samson, you're home, you're home! We've been searching all over for you. We were afraid we would never see you again."

Everyone was so pleased to see him safely back that no one remembered to scold him for leaving home by himself, and when Ben came around the corner from the dairy, milk pails in hand, he stopped and stared as though he couldn't believe his eyes.

"Well, would tha believe it?" he exclaimed, "the prodigal son's a' come 'ome. Gaw, tha give us all a turn, lad. We's thawt tha were dead, and instead thar tha was , oot 'avin a high old time b'tha self. Lookin' for a lady love, I'll wager! Haw,haw,haw," he cackled.

And that needs no translation.

Samson was so tired from all his adventures that he fell asleep immediately after he had greeted everybody. He had slept many hours and it was almost evening again when he was awakened by a strange noise. At first it seemed like ringing in his ears, and then a jumble of strange sounds – squeaks and grunts and whistles. Sleepily he sat up and scratched an ear with one back foot, and then scratched the other ear with his other back foot, but still the noise wouldn't go away.

Then, what had seemed like confusing sounds started to form words. They were not the kind of words you and I use, but all of a sudden, to Samson's great delight, he realized that he was on the Wildlife Telegraph and that he could understand the chatter of the inhabitants of the fields and woods. His excitement knew no bounds.

Soon a voice came through, loud and clear.

"Samson, this is Foxy. I want you to know that all your friends, and many other animals of the woods and fields, are gathered here at the edge of the Bluebell Woods to pay tribute to you. We are using the Wildlife Telegraph so we'll all be able to communicate with each other, and I have been elected Master of Ceremonies.

"I will begin by telling you that you are not only our beloved friend, but you are also our hero. You were a stranger in our midst, but you saved the lives of three of our wildlife sisters and you will never be forgotten by the field and woodland folk. You have proved yourself to be the true friend of all living creatures, and you are as brave and gallant as any of the knights who lived within the walls of your castle in years gone by."

Foxy sounded quaintly pompous and out of character as he made his speech of appreciation, but he received loud applause from his audience, and Samson was quite overwhelmed with surprise and delight at what he was hearing.

Foxy continued by saying, "Because of your kindness and compassion you have taught us all something that perhaps we never realized about ourselves. It has been an honor to know you."

Then, returning to his usual carefree manner of speech, he sang out, "Marty, you're on."

In his squeaky little voice, Marty began:

"Samson, I want you to know that I will never forget your kindness. When I was lost in the dungeon I was so frightened I thought I was going to die. Then you came. You didn't even know who I was but you comforted me, and then you carried me to safety. You really cared."

With a nervous little cough he finished with, "I know I can never be bold like you, Sam, but I'm going to learn not to let things frighten me any more – not even George!"

A tiny voice followed Marty's words:

"This is Beauty and I owe my life to you. I don't believe you even knew how to swim, and yet you jumped into the lake to save me. You are the bravest of anyone I have ever met and I know the knights your mother told you about would be proud of you. I am small and delicate so I can never be brave like you, but you have taught me what courage really is."

There was a fluttering of little wings as Beauty finished her speech, then a croaky voice came over the air waves.

"I hate to admit it, but I am just a rude, grumpy old frog who has no patience with anyone. I like to have my own way, and if I don't get it I throw a tantrum. Samson, you were so polite and patient you have made me feel very ashamed of myself. I really will try to follow your example and be a better frog in the future. Take care of yourself, we all love you."

Froggy sounded so choked up with emotion that Samson felt sorry for him. He would have liked to comfort the poor old fellow, but he didn't get the chance. Almost before Froggy had finished his doleful apology there was a familiar thumping over the Wildlife Telegraph. This was followed by a high-pitched little voice filled with excitement. The irrepressible Bunny could hardly contain herself.

"Oh, Samson, my hero! I would like to give you a big hug and thank you again and again for saving my life. You told me that you wanted to be strong and brave like the knights of long ago. I am only a silly young rabbit, and I don't even know what a knight is, but I think you are the strongest and bravest of anyone in all the whole wide world."

Then Bunny's voice dropped an octave or two and she sounded very solemn.

"I know now that I should have been good and listened to my mother, and others in the rabbit colony who are wiser than I am. I was told not to go near that hedge and I was disobedient because I thought it would be fun. I deserved what I got and it's only because of you that I am still alive. I'll never be able to thank you enough," she ended, with a little catch in her throat as she blew imaginary kisses at Samson.

Almost immediately a scratchy sound was heard coming over the Wild Life Telegraph, as though someone had taken a bristle brush and was scraping the wires.

"Hello, this is Mrs. Prickles speaking. Froggy just about said it all. I, too, can be rude and impatient, and I'm usually sorry afterwards. You were so polite and respectful to an old lady that it has made me realize just how bad tempered and selfish I can be. Please forgive me, Samson, and come back to see me whenever you can. You can share my space any time" she concluded.

A pleasant, cultured voice was heard next on the Wildlife Telegraph.

"This is Stinky, Samson. I want you to know that you have helped to change my life because you gave me the self-respect I needed. I have always kept to myself, but I try to find out how the rest of the world lives. That is how I know about my relatives in far off lands, and that we are all hated because we are different. We are born to defend ourselves in a manner that is obnoxious to humans and even to other animals, but you accepted me just the way I am, and I love you for it. You are my friend forever."

There was a short pause as Stinky's voice wavered a little, then an audible gulp as he recovered his composure.

"You are my hero, too, Samson. You are a good fellow and I will always cherish having known you," he said, with such emotion that Samson thought the polecat might burst into tears at any moment.

Samson just had time to say, "I love you too, Stinky," before Angel began to coo in such a gentle, soft voice that Samson could barely hear her.

"I probably owe you more than anyone." she began. "You didn't know me either, yet you were ready to sacrifice your own life for me. You were badly hurt and you still saved me. I can't think of anything braver than that. You told me that you wanted to rescue damsels in distress. Well, you rescued me and Bunny, and Beauty. We may not be the kind of damsels that were rescued by the knights, but we were in distress and our lives were in danger. And even if you don't wear shining armor and ride a big white charger you're still our brave knight. You are good, and kind, and courageous – everything a knight should be."

Samson was so impressed by all the speeches and the outpouring of love and admiration that he was completely at a loss for words. All he could manage to stammer was a short "Thank you, all my dear friends," then lapsed into a stunned silence as Foxy's voice returned to the Wildlife Telegraph in the same grandiose manner.

"My dear friend, Samson, we all got together and decided that we owe you some sort of recognition for your gallant deeds. In the tradition you described to me and to Angel, by popular consent of the dwellers in the woods and fields and streams, we have agreed that you deserve to be knighted. As there is no king or queen available to tap you on the shoulder with a sword and pronounce you "Sir Samson" we are taking it upon ourselves to award you this honor. So from now on you are "Sir Samson of Bluebell Woods." The sound of loud cheering and thumping of paws came over the Wildlife Telegraph before Foxy continued with his speech.

"Congratulations, my dear friend, but there is one more thing I have to say on behalf of myself and my colleagues. We decided unanimously that some kind of memento was appropriate so that you will never be forgotten. It so happened that Beaver was in his home on the lake when you plunged into the water to rescue Beauty. He witnessed your heroic deed.

"There is no finer woodworker than Beaver, and he has offered to carve you a plaque so that all the wildlife folk will remember you and your bravery." There was another round of applause and thumping of feet. Little voices were raised in the form of squeaks and squawks and grunts of approval.

When all the noise died down, Foxy continued. "There is a two hundred-year-old oak tree on the south side of the lake and I know she would be proud to display the plaque amongst her branches. Squirrel, who lives in the tree, will make sure it is secure and well hidden from humans.

"There are many good and kind humans, but there are others who would like to harm us, so we must be very cautious. For this reason we beg you not to tell the farm animals - and not even your mother - about anything that happened in the woods yesterday. It will be our secret, Sam, that will live forever in our hearts."

Samson was awestruck. He thought he must be dreaming, and that he would wake up at any minute to find himself alone in the loose box. Then he was brought back to reality by a chorus of "Speech! Speech!" and a stamping of little feet. Realizing that this clearly was not a dream, and embarrassed though he was, Samson felt obliged to say a few words.

"My very dear friends, I am so happy and overwhelmed by all of this that I don't know what to say, except to tell you that you have made all my dreams come true. I agree that this should be a secret and I would never risk harming you by revealing to anyone else what took place yesterday. I promise you that not even my mother will know what happened between me and the wildlife community, and all the wonderful friends I have made. So thank you from the bottom of my heart. I love every one of you."

Then all was silent, and at last Samson was alone to bask in his fame. Not a sound was heard but his own heart beating with excitement as he lay re-living all the wonderful things that had happened in the past twenty-four hours. Samson, being an unusually intelligent and well-informed young sheepdog (mainly due to his mother's tales) realized that in those few hours he had gained a lifetime of knowledge and understanding from the wild folk of the fields and woods and streams.

*****

You may think it sad that none of the farm animals, or Ben, or those who lived in the castle, would ever know that Samson was a hero, but Samson didn't care. Everyone at the castle and the home farm loved him, and even if he wasn't like the knights of old his mother couldn't have been prouder of him or loved him more. In any case, he found it rather exciting to keep such an important secret that was known only to himself and the wildlife folk. It made him feel extra special. And, if you are very quiet, one warm summer evening you just might see a large, furry Old English Sheepdog sitting under a two hundred-year-old oak tree by the lake, surrounded by a little bevy of wild folk. With a big smile on his face Samson gazes proudly up at a plaque that only he and the field and woodland dwellers can see. It reads:

SIR SAMSON OF BLUEBELL WOODS

OUR HERO

THE END

ABOUT THE AUTHOR

Monica Agnew-Kinnaman was born in England and came to America after serving in a British anti-aircraft artillery regiment during World War II. Although she had dogs all her life, since her husband died the last fifteen years have been devoted to taking old, abused and abandoned dogs that nobody wanted, so they can end their days in peace and comfort, and with lots of love. She has a doctorate in Psychology but is now retired. She lives in Colorado with Jess, her Border Collie. She also has a son and daughter who live in Colorado.

ABOUT THE ILLUSTRATOR

To view more of Diane Vallejo's artwork, follow her on Instagram @dkvallejoartist

If you have enjoyed this book, we hope you will enjoy the entire Samson's Adventures series:

The Adventures of Samson
The Further Adventures of Samson
Samson Goes to America

Other books by this author:
So This is Heaven: How Rescuing Old or Unwanted Dogs Provided a Touch of Heaven on Earth

61681917R00040

Made in the USA
Middletown, DE
20 August 2019